Tad-cu's Bobble Hat

MALACHY DOYLE

Illustrated by Dorry Spikes

for Daniel

I'll never forget the day I climbed
Foel Goch with Tad-cu Wil.
Up we went, hand in hand,
and when we got to the top –

Wowzer!

But Tad-cu said we had to go back down, double quick.

I started shivering, so he passed me his bobble hat
(the one with CYMRU on).

But I think Tad-cu was cold too.
He pulled up his hoody,
and he was coughing and coughing,
even more than usual.

The sun came out on the way down.
So I took off my Tad-cu's hat
and stuffed it into my pocket.

But when I got to the bottom,
I couldn't find it anywhere.
'I'm very sorry, Tad-cu.
I think I must have lost your bobble hat.'
'Never mind, bach,' he said.
'You'll find it another day.
There's always another day.'

When we got home, he went for a little lie-down.
Mam heated up some cawl, to warm me up.

Then she told me my Tad-cu
had had that hat since he was a boy!
That his very own Nain had knitted it for him!

So it was Mam who came with me,
back to the mountain the very next day,
to try and find my Tad-cu's bobble hat.

There'd been more snow, though –
much more snow –
and we couldn't see it anywhere.

It snowed and snowed that winter.
Tad-cu Wil coughed and coughed
in the bedroom next to mine.

By the time the snow finally melted,
the coughing had stopped
and the house was silent.

Mam and I went back up Foel Goch.
We really needed that bobble hat, see.

'We'd better go home, cariad,' said Mam.
'It'll be dark soon.'
But I wouldn't. Not without the hat.

And then I saw it!
It was peeping out from under a rock!
'Look, Mam! There it is! It's Tad-cu Wil's bobble hat!'

It was still a bit soggy,
but I tugged it down over my ears anyway.
Because I **love** that bobble hat!
It was made by my mam's dad's mam's mam –

Wowzers!

Yes, it's my lovely Tad-cu's bobble hat.
And it helps me remember him,
and all the mega times we had together.

So I wear it all the time now!
And I'm never going to lose it again,
I promise.

First published 2014 by Gomer Press, Llandysul, Ceredigion SA44 4JL

ISBN 978 1 84851 826 1

This book is published with the financial support of the Welsh Books Council.

Printed and bound in Wales at Gomer Press, Llandysul, Ceredigion
Wasg Gomer, Llandysul, Ceredigion SA44 4JL